For Gavin, the teacher

SIMON & SCHUSTER BOOKS FOR YOUNG READERS
An imprint of Simon & Schuster Children's Publishing Division
1230 Avenue of the Americas, New York, New York 10020

For information about special discounts for bulk purchases, please contact Simon &
Schuster Special Sales at 1-866-506-1949 or business@simonandschuster.com.
The Simon & Schuster Speakers Bureau can bring authors to your live event. For more
information or to book an event, contact the Simon & Schuster Speakers Bureau at
1-866-248-3049 or visit our website at www.simonspeakers.com.
Book design by Chloë Foglia • The text for this book is set in Barcelona.
The illustrations for this book are rendered using a combination of gouache and Photoshop.
Manufactured in China • 1115 SCP
2 4 6 8 10 9 7 5 3 1
Library of Congress Cataloging-in-Publication Data
Anstee, Ashlyn, author, illustrator. • No, no, Gnome! / Ashlyn Anstee. — First edition.
pages cm
Summary: "Gnome cannot wait to help his friends harvest the school garden! But his
eagerness and excitement get him into trouble, leaving them all saying 'No, no, Gnome!'"
—Provided by publisher.
ISBN 978-1-4814-3091-3 (hardcover : alk. paper) • ISBN 978-1-4814-3092-0 (eBook)
(1. Gnomes—Fiction. 2. Helpfulness—Fiction. 3. Gardening—Fiction. 4. Schools—Fiction.)
I. Title. • PZ7.1.A575No 2016 • (E)—dc23 • 2015003893

No, No, Gnome!

ashlyn anstee

Simon & Schuster Books for Young Readers
New York London Toronto Sydney New Delhi

The students at Greenthumb Elementary had been working hard on their garden all year long.

Finally it was almost ready to harvest!
Everyone was excited.

Especially Gnome.

As the students headed outside, Mr. Waters assigned each of them a task.

The kids quickly got to work.

At first, Gnome was helpful.

But then . . .

Mr. Waters suggested
Gnome try something else.

But pretty soon . . .

Mr. Waters gave Gnome
one last chance.

All Gnome had to do was stand still and hold the basket for the garden clippings.

But Gnome didn't even last one minute.

Mr. Waters sent Gnome
back to the classroom.

When the other kids returned,
no one said hello.

At recess, no one
would play with him.

And at the end of the day,
no one said good-bye.

Gnome
was
blue.

How could he show his friends
that he was sorry?

The next day, Gnome couldn't wait to get back to the garden.

The other kids were dreading it.

But when they went outside . . .

The students got to work picking their harvest bounty. Gnome was helpful.

Most of the time.